Books by Sheila Greenwald

ALL THE WAY TO WIT'S END
IT ALL BEGAN WITH JANE EYRE:
  Or, The Secret Life of Franny Dillman
GIVE US A GREAT BIG SMILE, ROSY COLE
BLISSFUL JOY AND THE SATs
  A Multiple-Choice Romance
WILL THE REAL GERTRUDE HOLLINGS
  PLEASE STAND UP?
VALENTINE ROSY

Valentine Rosy

Valentine Rosy

Sheila Greenwald

An Atlantic Monthly Press Book
Little, Brown and Company
BOSTON   TORONTO

Third Printing

Library of Congress Cataloging in Publication Data

Greenwald, Sheila.
  Valentine Rosy.

  "An Atlantic Monthly Press Book."
  Summary: When eleven-year-old Rosy's friend Hermione announces that Rosy is having a Valentine's party, a dismayed Rosy finds herself in unwilling competition with the sophisticated Christi who is planning an exclusive party on the same day.
  1. Children's stories, American. [1. Parties — Fiction. 2. Valentine's Day — Fiction. 3. Schools — Fiction. 4. New York (N.Y.) — Fiction] I. Title.
  PZ7.G852Val 1984   [Fic]   84-9694
  ISBN 0-316-32708-5

ATLANTIC—LITTLE, BROWN BOOKS
ARE PUBLISHED BY
LITTLE, BROWN AND COMPANY
IN ASSOCIATION WITH
THE ATLANTIC MONTHLY PRESS

MV

Published simultaneously in Canada
by Little, Brown & Company (Canada) Limited

PRINTED IN THE UNITED STATES OF AMERICA

For my aunts
Eddy
Gertie
Helen and
Lil

♥ Chapter One

My name is Rosy Cole. I have two older sisters named Anitra and Pippa, a mother and father named Sue and Mike, a cat named Pie, and an uncle Ralph, who is a successful photographer.

Here is a photograph that Uncle Ralph took of us one year ago.

My sister Anitra is fourteen. She used to study ballet. Four years ago, when she was ten, Uncle Ralph did a book about her. It was called *Anitra Dances*. It featured photographs of my sister looking cute and adorable in her tutu and leotard.

My sister Anitra at 10.

Now Anitra plays drums with Jaded
Jay and the Putrids.

My sister Pippa is thirteen. She used to love to ride horses. Three years ago, when she was ten, Uncle Ralph did a book all about Pippa. It showed beautiful photographs of Pippa in horse shows, jumping and galloping.

My sister
Pippa
at 10

Pippa has switched to electric guitar.
She plays with Jaded Jay and the Putrids
too.

Uncle Ralph never got a book out of me
(I won't go into it); but he did get a wife.
Aunt Teddy was my violin teacher.

One month ago, when I turned eleven, Mom had a party for me at home. Uncle Ralph took out the Nikon to pose us for the family portrait.

"Hey, Sis," he said. "I've got an idea for a new book on Anitra and Pippa."

"*Anitra Bangs and Pippa Twangs?*" Daddy joked.

"No," Ralph said, *"Rage and Rebellion in the Adolescent Child."*

"I don't like it," Mom said.

"That is because you cannot confront the truth," Pippa snapped.

"Oh," Mom moaned, "here we go again. What happened anyway? One year ago, I had these three darling children. A Dancer, a Rider, and a ten-year-old. Now I have Rage and Rebellion and a . . . a . . ." She looked at me.

"An eleven-year-old," I reminded her.

"What happened?" Mom repeated.

I couldn't blame her for asking. The change in our family had been so sudden. It was as if a Reverse Fairy Godmother had waved an upside-down wand over my pretty, perfect sisters and turned them into sulky slobs overnight.

"Do you really want to know?" Anitra asked Mom.

Ralph focused his camera on her. "Could you just hold that look of disgust and contempt for another minute, sweetheart?"

"Ralph, in another minute I will ask you to leave." Mom slammed down her cake fork.

"But, Sis, these girls are going through a phase every kid goes through. If I handle it right, it could be a best-seller. We could do the talk shows with a coast-to-coast hook-up."

"Those girls shouldn't be on talk shows," Aunt Teddy said. "They should be on Keep Quiet shows until they learn to behave."

"You treated us as if we were your puppets and dolls," Anitra accused Mom. "You pushed us around. Dancing classes, riding lessons, shows, auditions. Rosy was the only one with the brains to refuse. She taught us a lesson. If you were so interested in fame, why didn't you make your own thrilling life?"

"Because I had to work five days a week in an office full of lawyers to help pay for the costumes and lessons and tutors that were necessary to build careers for you girls."

"Who asked you?" Pippa's eyes filled with tears. "We never had a choice."

At the moment, neither did I. If we had been in a restaurant, I could have hidden in the ladies' room, or gone home. But I *was* home. Even on my birthday, home

12

was like Amateur Fight Night at the Garden. It was my sisters against my mother with my father as referee and Uncle Ralph taking pictures for posterity.

"Could you wave your fist in the air again, honey? I don't think I caught that," he asked Pippa.

I tapped my water glass and called, "Round One."

Nobody heard.

Daddy took Mom's hand. "What Sue needs is a vacation. We're going away, just the two of us, for Valentine's Day weekend."

"That's a whole month from now," Mom said. "I hope I make it."

"Oh boy." Anitra winked at Pippa. "I hope so too."

There was something about that wink that bothered me, but Uncle Ralph loved it. "Hey, do that again," he told Anitra. "It looks cute."

Cute? I thought it looked like trouble.

Ralph leveled his viewfinder on me. "Say, Birthday Girl, what did you wish for when you blew out those candles?"

It was my big chance. I took a deep

breath and stood up. "I wished for One Big Happy Family."

For a minute, everybody froze, then Pippa shook her head and laughed. "You just turned eleven, Rosy, but you sound like five. One Big Happy Family? You must be kidding. There is no such thing. I can't even imagine it."

I could. In fact, what I imagined could make my uncle's most beautiful photographic book yet. Not the one about The Dancer, or The Rider, or A Little Fiddler, but about all five of us. Mom, Dad, Pippa, Anitra, and Me singing around the piano, baking bread, playing word games, sharing, loving and trusting in soft focus through a yellow filter . . .

Pippa glared at me, and the imaginary book snapped shut. "Since you told us your wish, you've ruined your chance of getting it," she said.

"Don't blame Rosy," Anitra came to my defense. "It isn't her fault that we changed and grew up. She's about to change and grow up herself."

"Rage and Rebellion, Part Three?" Daddy looked at me in horror.

Mom turned pale and I heard her murmur, "Not again."

"Oh no, I won't," I promised them. "Not me. I won't change and grow."

And I meant it.

At least I thought I did.

♥ *Chapter Two*

When I met Hermione Wong the next morning in the lobby, she said, "So, how was that family-only birthday party?"

I could tell she was still annoyed because I hadn't asked her. Hermione waits for me in the lobby of the building where we both live so we can walk to school together. We're in the same class. I was about to tell her a made-up story about my One Big Happy Family when the elevator door opened and out stepped Christi McCurry.

You have to see her to believe her, and even then it isn't easy. It seems impossible that it was only three months ago that I saw Christi for the first time. I was in the kitchen fixing cocoa when I noticed that new people were carrying furniture into the apartment across the courtyard. In the window where Chucky Coopersmith used to launch water bombs, something else was going on.

I buzzed Hermione to come right over.

Hermione said, "She's a model. I'll bet you anything."

"Look at all that makeup," I pointed.

Hermione shook her head. "Poor thing has to cover about two million wrinkles. Models are over the hill by the time they hit twenty-five."

The next day we met her.

We had guessed right about her being a model and wrong about her two million wrinkles. What we never would have guessed in two *zillion* years was that she was eleven and a half and headed for our fifth grade at the Read School.

Read is a small private school for girls on the Upper East Side of Manhattan. It was founded by Miss Augusta Read about fifty years ago. We wear uniforms to school because Miss Read believed that uniforms encourage modesty and decorum. In spite of the uniform, Read tries to develop individual thought. "Let them conform in their dress so that their minds may be free," Miss Read wrote in the school handbook under "philosophy."

Here is a picture of our class last year in our uniforms and free minds.

Here is our class picture this year in our uniforms. I don't know about the free minds anymore.

Maybe you can tell that we've become two groups.

In my group there is me, Hermione, Debbie Prusock, Wendy Ash and Linda Dildine. In Christi's group there is everybody else. They have all changed their names to end with an *i*. They call themselves the Christi-Belles. We don't call ourselves anything.

They call us the Babies.

The only time we forget our groups is in chorus. Mrs. Forrest tells us where to stand. "Sopranos in the front and altos behind them." Then she waves her arms, "One, Two, Three," and Linda Dildine plays the opening chords and Mrs. Forrest cries out, "Everybody together now."

And we are. When we sing all our voices join as if to tell us what it could be like if we were friends. Right now we are rehearsing for the spring assembly that we do with our brother school, Finchley. Our songs are " 'Tis a Gift to Be Simple" and "Chairs to Mend." One is an old Shaker tune and the other a peddler's chant. "Chairs to mend, oh chairs to mend. Mackerel, fresh mackerel." But as soon as chorus is over, it's back to Christi-Belles and Babies.

Christi walks to school with Hermione and me only because we all happen to be going in the same direction. The walks always make Hermione nervous. I could see her starting to get tense that morning as soon as we saw Christi step out of the elevator.

"How do you get to be a movie star?" Hermione didn't lose a minute.

"Once I have become famous as a top-flight model, I will launch my career in film. I have a manager who is guiding me. He sees to it that I get proper exposure. Good management is key."

"Exactly." Hermione nodded. "I couldn't agree more."

At that moment I realized something, and it didn't make me feel too good. The only reason Hermione Wong was one of

us Babies was because she couldn't figure out how to be a Christi-Belle.

Just as we turned the corner from Park Avenue heading east, somebody called out, "Hi Christi, how ya doin'?"

It was Charley Hicks. He was with Mickey Buttonwiser and Lucas Ash, Wendy's brother. They go to Finchley. When I was very young I played in the same sandbox as Charley and Lucas. Once we made sandburgers and tried to eat them. Once we built a pyramid we could almost live inside of. Once we buried a treasure and then couldn't find it.

Christi sucked in her cheeks and rolled her eyes. "They're sweet, but kind of young."

"I couldn't agree more." Hermione nodded again. She was beginning to look like one of those dogs people put in the back window of their car that keep nodding.

The three boys crossed the street to walk

with us. Actually, walking with *us* isn't
exactly an accurate description.

"I have you down on my list," Christi
said, beaming a smile from Charley to
Lucas to Mickey.

25

"What list?" they responded together, like the Finchley fifth-grade chorus.

"My list of the boys I like," Christi explained. "I keep a list of the boys I like on the back of my notebook. All three of you are on it, but I can't tell you which numbers you are."

"What do you mean, which numbers?" Charley said.

"Well, somebody has to be first and somebody second and then somebody has to be last."

"Am I last?" Mickey looked as if he were about to be sick.

"I cannot tell." Christi shut her eyes. "But don't despair. I assure you that all three of you are invited to my Valentine's party: numbers one through ten."

"Does that include us?" Hermione whispered.

"What do you think?" I said.

"I'll find out." I noticed Hermione's eyes

were crossing the way they do when she gets upset.

All through math, I saw Hermione writing and crossing things out and chewing on the end of her eraser.

"Hermione Wong, what are you doing?" Mrs. Oliphant said. "You haven't looked at the board once." She picked up Hermione's notebook and began to read. "Mickey Buttonwiser, Bobby Tobin, Ezra Pinkwater? Are these fractions?"

Everybody giggled, and Hermione's face looked like cranberries.

When Mrs. Oliphant went back to the blackboard, I saw Christi pass her list to Mari Settleheim and then Mari Settleheim pass her list to Jenni Gilchrist. Only they didn't get caught. Maybe that was the difference between a Christi-Belle and a Baby.

After class Mrs. Oliphant returned Hermione's list to her. "I know boys are interesting," she said, "but they won't help you out on Friday's fraction test."

As far as I could tell, they couldn't help you out on anything. What was going on, anyway? Why was Hermione making some dumb list of boys at the back of her notebook? Why were Charley and Lucas and Mickey falling over themselves trying to find out what number they were on Christi's list? Lucas Ash, my old buddy, plays Monopoly the same way I do: for blood. I thought we understood each other. I began to think I was wrong.

In the lunchroom there are two tables.
As usual all ten Christi-Belles squeezed
in at one, and us five Babies sat at the
other.

Except for Hermione.

She more or less swayed in between.

Everyone at our table was trying not to chew so we wouldn't miss a word of what the Christi-Belles had to say on the subject of lipstick.

"I just love Flamingo Flame Lip Quencher, don't you, Christi?" we heard Mari Settleheim say.

"It's too orangy for my skin tone." Christi shook her curls. "It makes me look sallow unless I use a lot of blusher."

"My boyfriend likes it," Mari pouted.

"My boyfriend . . ." Hermione let her chair screech down. ". . . he likes Root Beer Lip Treat."

"Root Beer Lip Treat?" Christi's brows went up and she snorted in a way that made me think she knew Hermione never had a boyfriend and had in fact accidentally eaten her Root Beer Lip Treat going up on the ski lift at Killington last Christmas.

"It's like a training lipstick." Jenni Gilchrist yawned.

"Unless you combine it with vanilla ice cream." Natali Pringle giggled.

Hermione began to rock back and forth again, only this time she looked dangerous, like an unguided missile about to land on something. "Hey, Christi, you never told me when your Valentine's party is."

"My Valentine's party?" Christi blinked. "It's on Valentine's Day. But I'm so sorry, dear . . ." (she sure looked it)

". . . everybody is paired up already."

"What does that mean?"

"Dated."

Hermione stopped rocking. I closed my eyes. I was sure she would crash. "I couldn't come anyway," she said. "I'm invited to another party."

"Whose party is that?"

"Rosy's." She flipped her hair over one shoulder.

Debbie Prusock sucked in air and looked over at me. "Rosy who?"

"Rosy Cole, you wimp." Hermione stood up, grabbed her lunchbox, and beat it.

I was wrong. *She* hadn't crashed.

I had.

I couldn't find her for the rest of the afternoon. She left school before I did. I caught a glimpse of her running two blocks ahead of me, with her jacket flapping and her knapsack open.

I followed her home.

"Can't open the door." She coughed. "I have a fever."

"And I have a Valentine's party." I put my mouth to the Medico lock. "I'd like to know how come."

"Because I'm sick and tired of being a dumb Baby. I want to make *them* jealous for a change. You ought to thank me, Rosamond." I could hear her put the chain on the door. "If you have a party for all us Babies, it will change your image. I set you up to give the party, because you are my special friend, and that is what Valentine's Day is all about. I am knocking my brains out to give you status. And do you ever thank me for it? Do you ever do anything nice for me in return?"

"Thanks a lot, Hermione," I said, "but I can't have a party. My parents will be away."

"Then pretend you're having a party. Make believe, the way we do when we play Famous Opera Star."

All of a sudden I really did feel like a baby. "We get dressed up to play, the way the Christi-Belles get dressed for real life. I'm sick of pretending."

I heard the chain come off the inside lock.

"You are?"

"I'll ask permission for a real party."

"Oh, Rosy."

"I'll have cake and ice cream and a big paper heart and Linda and Debbie and Wendy."

"And we won't be the Babies."

"And we won't be the Christi-Belles either. We'll be us again. Rose and Hermione."

"Actually, Rose . . ." Hermione opened the door. She was wearing her mother's fur boa and pearls. "I'm changing my name. From now on please call me Hermi."

Chapter Three

The next morning Hermi was not waiting for me in the lobby. Instead she was standing by the outside door in a strong wind, shivering.

"I thought I needed a little fresh air." She looked over my shoulder at the elevator. I knew she was really waiting for Christi. "Why don't you walk ahead of me? I wouldn't dream of slowing you down."

I was about to say a few words on the subject of loyalty when Christi appeared.

"How are your party plans, Baby Rose?" she drawled.

"I'm buying the invitations this after-noon," I said.

"What will you put on them?"

"The date, the time and the place." I wondered what I had left out, because Christi was smirking.

"What about the live entertainment?" Hermione nudged me. "Aren't you going to put that down?"

"That will be a surprise." It certainly would. I had a sinking feeling it would end up being Hermione on cello.

"Anybody can hire a magician, Infant," Christi said. "But not anybody can get really neat boys. What boys will be at Baby Rose's Bash?"

"The boys are a surprise, too," I said.

BOYS?

The surprise was that I needed any. It hadn't even dawned on me. I had no idea how to find them, and less of how to get them to come.

Even Hermi was completely silent.

Later Hermione grabbed me in the locker room. "Put on your coat and meet me by the first-floor bench as soon as you're ready."

"Don't you have a cello lesson?"

"For your information, Rose, my cello is part of my past life," Hermione paused. "And you will be too if you keep me waiting."

I met her by the hall bench and followed her into Central Park without asking any questions. Was this a treasure hunt? We jumped over the wall near the entrance on Ninetieth Street. At the bottom of a small hill behind a clump of shrubs were all the Christi-Belles. There were also Peter Loomis and Marty Moorman from Finchley's seventh grade. Peter acts in school plays and Marty does imitations. Was it a rehearsal for a skit?

"Christi invited me to watch the Belles in action," Hermione whispered. "She said

I could bring you along if you don't tell the other Babies."

"Tell them what?"

"What you are about to see."

"What am I about to see?"

"Pay attention."

The Christi-Belles lined up like the Rockettes, only they weren't dancing. I wished I wasn't standing there, hiding behind a tree in the freezing cold. Even faking it on my violin at Aunt Teddy's School of Music while she screamed "Idiot" at me would be better. "What do you call this, a recital?" I whispered.

"Kissing Demonstration," Hermione hissed.

"Isn't it romantic?"

41

Here's how it worked. Peter went down the row of Belles, kissing each one of them for exactly a minute. It was exactly a minute because Marty held a stopwatch and called "time." Christi kept score in her famous notebook.

"Mari Settleheim, you got an eight."

"Why?"

"For opening your eyes and honking through your nose."

"I have a cold."

Peter looked upset and wiped off his mouth. "I don't want your cold. Next time you better tell me first."

"Listen, Hermi," I whispered. "I thought romantic meant you really like the person you're kissing and so you have a lot of feelings about it."

"Don't be stupid. Peter isn't even on Christi's list. They are just kissing for practice."

"I thought practice was what you do on the violin or cello."

"How would you know?" She gave me a nasty look. "Honestly, Rose, why don't you grow up?"

When the Kissing Demonstration was over we walked out of the park. Hermione went to Aunt Teddy's for her cello lesson and I went to Gimbel's to Grow Up.

I love Gimbel's.

I love the way the lights and the smells and the warmth fold around you the minute you walk in the door, like a hug. I wish Gimbel's was my home. When I was young I visited the television floor and the toy department, but today was different. Today was serious. If I handled it right, I'd grow up enough to impress the Christi-Belles and get my mother's permission for a party.

I walked past jewelry, veered left at

handbags, and there I was. Miles of trays and jars and tubes and tubs and sticks and powders and creams. How would I get through it? The salesladies all looked like lab technicians. It was hopeless. I was really about to leave, when I saw something amazing. It was almost as if they were waiting for me.

There was Tender Rose, and Wild Rose and Jungle Rose, Enchanted Rose, Rose

Feather and Rose Fever. There was Innocent Rose (forget it) and Antique Rose (I didn't have to go overboard). First I tried Wet Rose. The taste was nice, but I looked as if I had been drinking blood. Then Frosted Rose. I had gotten the same effect once from a cold sore.

"Can I help you?" a saleslady asked me.

"I don't know which one to get."

"Alluring Rose is this year's color," she said.

"Then I'd better take it." That was all I needed, to be caught with last year's color on my mouth. It certainly wouldn't hurt if I were alluring.

After I bought the lipstick, I sprayed myself from five different toilet waters and rubbed body elixir up my arms and exfoliating cream on my chin and Magic Moisture on my neck and Liquid Dew on my nose. I even got some extract of the Queen Bee between my eyes.

Finally, when nothing would stick on me anymore, I headed to the Party Shop. At the Party Shop I bought a bag of heart-shaped balloons and a box of invitations with hearts all over the inside of the envelopes. I thought my parents would have a hard time saying no to my party when they saw all the preparations I was making.

As soon as I got home, I put on my Alluring Rose. It made my lips feel sticky and shiny. I was wondering if my mouth was alluring yet, when Pippa opened my door to ask if she could borrow my rubber cement. She was trying out a new hairdo.

"Good grief!" she shrieked. "What's the matter with you, Rose? You look so weird."

She covered her face so that I wouldn't notice she was laughing. *She* thought *I* looked funny.

"Rosy Posy, let me help you. I've had lots of experience with makeup. I could do you like awesome."

"I don't want to be awesome," I told her. "I just want to appear mature so Mom will give me permission for a Valentine's party while she's away."

"You want to have a party on Valentine's Day?" Pippa seemed upset.

"If they let me."

"Wait a minute, Rosy Cole." She put out her hand. "Don't move."

She rushed down the hall to find Anitra. Soon I heard them both outside my door. They were whispering. Then they burst in.

"Rosy dearest, guess what?"

"We will chaperone your party for you."

They sat beside me on my bed and gave me little hugs. I could tell they were really trying to be nice.

"You see, Rosy," Anitra said, "we were already planning to have a couple of friends over on Valentine's Day. We didn't want to tell Mom. We knew she would worry. But if she gives you permission for a little party and lets us be your chaperones and finds out later that one or two of our friends stopped in, she won't feel that we deceived her. It works out for all of us."

"And don't you worry about our not being chaperone types," Anitra said, as though she'd been reading my mind. "Just wait."

A little later when they came in to dinner, I saw the Reverse Fairy Godmother had waved her wand again.

Anitra pirouetted to Mom on demi-pointe and kissed her cheek. "Love you," she said.

Pippa gave Daddy a hug. "Could you advance me some money? I would like to buy a hairpiece till my Mohawk grows in."

"Let's call it a gift, honey," Daddy cried. "And treat yourself to a whole wig."

"What's happened to you girls?" my mother exclaimed. "This is like a miracle. I wish Ralph were here to see it."

So did I.

Exit Rage and Rebellion.

Enter One Big Happy Family.

My party was in the bag.

Could boys be far behind?

Chapter Four

All of a sudden, Christi started waiting to walk to school with us in the morning. She was curious about my party.

"Have you found enough boys yet, Baby Rose?"

"Rose has more than enough boys," Hermione said.

"And the live entertainment?"

"There will be some cello selections and Rosy's sisters will do a few numbers."

"Actually, my sisters will be our chaperones." I just wanted to set things straight.

"Chaperones?" Christi wailed. "Oh you poor Babies."

"It's the name of their group." Hermione gave me a kick. "The Chaperones are fantastic. Not only do they sing, they dance too."

"Oh sure." Christi did an eye-roll. "Ring Around A Rosy."

Boys.

Where could I find them?

After school, to take my mind off my problems, I went right to Gimbel's. I rode the escalator and walked around.

I didn't know which of us was a bigger dummy.

When I got home Pippa showed me a package. "I bought something for your party." It was a Pin-the-Tail-on-the-Donkey.

"Thanks for taking such an interest, Pippa, but what I really need for my party is boys," I said.

"Boys?" Pippa looked amazed. "Rosy, you're only in the fifth grade."

"So what?"

"Don't grow up too fast, the way we did. Take advantage of being young. Don't try to be like that disgusting Christi Mc-Curry."

"Stop it," I practically screamed. "I'm not trying to be like Christi McCurry, but I'm sick of everyone treating me as if I were a baby. It seems the only way I can make them stop is to get boys to come to my party."

Pippa tried to say something, but I pushed her out of my room, slammed the door, and threw the stupid Pin-the-Tail-on-the-Stupid-Donkey at it.

I looked at the stack of invitations. Debbie Prusock, Wendy Ash, Linda Dildine, Hermione and me. The Babies. I was running out of time. Less than three weeks to go. I needed a brainstorm. I got out my notebook.

Brainstorms

1. Put a sign on Christi's Door.

```
QUARANTINE
Do NOT ENTER
            Dept of
            Health
```

2. Put a sign on MY Door

```
BOYS
ROOM
```
Ha!

3. Learn to fly like Wonder Woman and scoop up bunches of boys as if they were overcoats.

4. Maybe I am a baby. Maybe this is hopeless

5.

I was trying to come up with number five when Wendy Ash called. She was very excited. "Will the boys at your party buy us corsages and pick us up in a taxi and take us home in a taxi?"

Was she kidding?

"Because Lucas has to do that for his date when he goes to Christi's party." She began to whisper. "He's furious. It means he needs an advance on his allowance if he can get it and even then he won't be able to buy a pizza till April."

"May," Lucas corrected her on the extension.

"I'm sorry, Lucas," I said. "I wish I could help, but I have problems of my own just now."

"If only it was like Monopoly," he sighed, "with piles of fake bills and deals you can make on hotels and houses."

"I know what you mean," I agreed. "A party isn't like Monopoly."

"No," he said. "Monopoly is fun."

To make matters worse, Anitra and Pippa began to take over my party.

"I'm going to put on my costume from the Nutcracker and perform a solo," Anitra told my parents at dinner.

"Then we'll have lots of games to play and lovely food. A heart-shaped cake with pink icing and pink punch."

"Every girl will get a little nosegay of tea roses and pink carnation to pin on her dress."

"It sounds like the most perfect party a group of fifth-grade girls could hope for." Mom smiled. "Ballet, pastry, punch, and flowers. It's just a dream."

It sounded more like a nightmare to me. I had a baby party with baby games and no boys. I had my sisters to chaperone. And I had the Christi-Belles waiting for me to make an idiot of us all.

The countdown to my party continued, and there was no hope in sight.

Then Hermione had an idea.

"Remember, Rosy, you once advertised for signatures in the park when you wanted to get out of taking violin lessons?"

"Yes, I remember."

"Well?"

"I'll get the sign ready," I said, "and pick you up in half an hour."

I really had to hand it to Hermione. I hurried over to thank her.

But when she opened her door, I forgot what I'd come for.

"It's my new image, Rose."

"What was wrong with the old one?"

"It was so young. I mean, really, Root Beer Lip Treat and Mary Janes."

"Did you eat your Mary Janes, too?" I laughed. "You should have eaten that eye gunk and that rouge while you were at it."

"This isn't rouge. It's highlighter. And it isn't eye gunk. It's Violet Smoke shadow, and for your information you look like you belong to the Kindergarten Club. I am really very sorry for you, Rose. You obviously have a problem about growing up. I keep trying to help you. But you won't accept my help. One look at you and no one will sign up for your party. Quite frankly, I don't blame them. I wouldn't be seen in the park with you." She stared at me as if I were her cello and closed the door in my face.

This was not the first disagreement I ever had with Hermione, but it was the most upsetting. Maybe she was right. Maybe I was scared to grow up. I took my poster home and checked myself out. Hair . . . I didn't have the right kind, so I borrowed Pippa's wig. Good.

Eyes?
They needed to look bigger, also blue. Since they're brown, I put the blue on top.

Cheeks?
Pink,
very pink.

Something was still missing.

I could fix that, too.

Finally I was ready to take my poster to the Sheep Meadow in Central Park where Finchley was holding soccer practice. I leaned my sign against the tree where jackets and books had been dumped in a heap.

63

I thought at first nobody would sign up. But then Charley Hicks asked somebody for a pencil, and somebody else borrowed it from him, and then somebody borrowed it from him. I couldn't believe how easy it was. I had to laugh. Wait till I tell old Hermi.

When they had all left, I went to take down my sign.

IF YOU WOULD LIKE TO HAVE A GREAT TIME SIGN UP FOR ROSYS VALENTINE PARTY ♡ ♡

FOOD FLOWERS FUN PROVIDED FREE

NAME	ADRESS	Phone	Comments
KING KONG	EMPIRE STATE BUILDING	With MAYO on RYE	ArGhhh
BIG BAD WOOLF	GRANDMA'S HOUSE	With HAM on ROLL	what a nice wig you have
TYRAN ASAUR-US REX	MUSEUM NATURAL HISTORY	With KING KONG & Big Bad Woolf	YUM

On second thought, maybe I wouldn't tell Hermi.

65

As I walked out of the park, Lucas was waiting for me. "My father won't give me an advance on my allowance. That means I only have enough money for one corsage and one taxi ride, or two taxi rides and no corsage. Even then I don't eat pizza till May."

"Let your date take her own taxi. Meet her at Christi's," I suggested.

"What about the flowers?"

"What about them?"

"Your poster says you provide them free

at your party. A couple of us are wondering just how long we have to stay at your party for you to provide them."

"How many of you?"

"Ezra, Charley, Mike, Mickey, and Bobby."

"Half an hour."

"Sounds like a long time. How about ten minutes?"

"You can drink the punch."

"Can we watch TV?"

"Fifteen minutes."

"Deal."

I got tingly all over. I don't know if it was romantic. I don't know if it was grown up. Actually, it was a lot like Monopoly.

I had six boys for fifteen minutes apiece. Ninety minutes' worth of boys. Not bad. I dialed Hermione right away.

"What do you call that?" she said.

"I call it a beginning," I said. "Now all I need is a middle and an end."

♥ *Chapter Five*

The next day in math all I could think was, "Tomorrow is Valentine's Day." I got so nervous I had to go to the third-floor girls' room and run the taps. But Mari Settleheim was at my favorite sink doing a little water therapy of her own.

"What's the matter, Mari?" I asked.

"My party dress doesn't button. I put on weight. My date won't pick me up in a taxi."

"What difference does that make?"

"Oh, it'll make a difference all right, when the other Christi-Belles hear."

"They're probably all in the same boat," I said, feeling happy and guilty at the same time. "I'm certainly glad we don't have to worry about things like that at my party."

"That is because you don't have boys at your party," Mari said, "and so you don't even know how much fun you are missing."

I turned off the water. Talking to Mari had been better for my nerves than a gallon of water therapy. Suddenly I felt the way I do when I'm on a winning streak in Monopoly. When I've got piles of bills on my side of the board and hotels on Park Place and I'm the banker.

Saturday morning and Valentine's Day. My parents packed their overnight cases and kissed us good-bye. After they left, my sisters asked me to go down and pick up the cake and flowers they had ordered. When I came home, the mail was under our door. There was something for me.

Rose's are Red
Violets are Blue
I'd stay at your party
If I could
and That's TRUE
Lucas

I couldn't believe it. Lucas sent me a Valentine.

He liked me.
What would I do?
The important thing was,
what would I wear?
I ran to the closet to make myself look terrific. I tried on my recital dress from last year.

And my party dress from the
year before that. My closet was a dud. I
tried my mother's.

I put on her black taffeta waltz-length
skirt, which is floor-length on me, her
jewel-neck blouse, which is scoop-neck on
me, and her silk belt, which is very tight
on both of us.

Then I brushed my
hair up and sprayed it
and brushed it down
and sprayed it and put
her gold hoops in my
ears and Alluring Rose
on my mouth.

"How do you do?" I introduced myself.
"Ms. Rosamond Cole, hostess."

Help, it was almost time for my party. In the living room Anitra was setting up her drums and Pippa was plugging in her amplifier.

"Is that for when you dance the Nutcracker?"

"Dance the what?" They looked at me as if I were the nut.

"Dance the Nutcracker for my party?"

"*Your* party? Oh no. This is so we can jam at *our* party."

It was my turn to be confused.

"We told you we were having a few of our friends over, and you're our excuse."

"I was an excuse?"

"Remember, you said you wanted a grown-up party? Well, you're going to get one, Rosy Cole."

Just then the doorbell rang.

It was Jaded Jay and a few of his friends.

By the time the doorbell rang again, we could hardly hear it, so we left the door open.

Soon there was no room anywhere in the apartment. Somebody was in the shower. Somebody was in the beds. Somebody was shaving with Dad's razor. Somebody was putting on Mom's perfume. Somebody said to me, "I heard about this party on the bus. How did you hear about it?"

"I live here."

"Then maybe you ought to do something about those poor little kids in the kitchen."

Those poor little kids in the kitchen were my entire Valentine Party. I hadn't even seen them come in.

Lucas said, "Rosy, what's wrong with your mouth?"

"It's alluring."

"I never dreamed you'd have a party like this," Linda said.

"Like what?"

"Like the most incredible party ever," Hermione answered for Linda.

"With a real live combo," Ezra gasped. "Wow, Jaded Jay and the Putrids."

"Could we hang around when our fifteen minutes are up?" Charley asked.

"I suppose so." I went to the refrigerator to get the nosegays. On the way I happened to look out the window, across the courtyard. All the Christi-Belles were standing at Christi's window glaring at me. I watched Christi pick up her phone. She could have saved a dime. I was able to lip-read across the court.

"Rosy Cole, you have got the entire BOY part of my party over there. If you don't send them here immediately, we are coming to get them."

"The more the merrier," I said. "I've already got Jaded Jay and the Putrids and half of New York."

I hung up and shouted, "Christi's party is on the way."

"I don't believe it," Hermione whooped. "We won."

It was true. Here I was giving the most

terrific grown-up party of anybody in my entire class. Everybody in the kitchen knew it. When Christi and the Belles walked in a few minutes later, they knew it too.

I felt as if I were filling up like one of the heart-shaped balloons I had never bothered to blow up. I felt as if I were floating clear to the ceiling. "Come on, everybody." I waved my hands. "What are we hanging around in the kitchen for? Let's go join the fun."

They all followed me into the living room to join the fun.

Jaded Jay stopped playing.

"What's up, Putrid Pippa? Did Nurse send the Babies in to say good-night?"

"That's just our sister Rosy and a few of her friends," Pippa explained.

"They look like Halloween in the Play-pen."

"Why don't you kids go back to the kitchen?" Anitra said.

Back to the kitchen?

One minute I had the best party in New York and the next it was all over.

"Maybe we could go to Christi's now?" Linda asked.

"No we can't!" Christi was furious. "Nobody calls me a Baby. I'm a famous fashion model. He can't push me around."

"Hey wait," I told Anitra. "It isn't fair."

But she didn't seem to hear me. She had turned up her amplifier.

We trooped back to the kitchen single file, like a retreating army.

"What will we do?" Hermione whispered. "We can't stay holed up here all night. Your party is going to be kaput if you don't think of something fast, Rose."

"We should fight back," Lucas said.

"We have our rights."

"We have to tell them who we are and that they can't push us around."

"Who are we?" I asked them.

Nobody answered me. We stood and thought about it. I looked at us thinking about it, and it came to me. Right there between the sink and the refrigerator was more than half of the Finchley-Read fifth-grade chorus. I knew exactly what we had to do.

I gave everybody a wet paper towel, and my comb and brush, and went back to talk to Jaded Jay and Anitra and Pippa.

"We want a turn at the piano," I said. "Don't forget, as far as Mom knows, this is my party." If this sounded like a threat, it's entirely possible that's what it was.

Anitra and Pippa shrugged at each other, and then at Jay.

"It's okay with me," he said. "We could use a break."

Linda Dildine sat at the piano. We all knew where to stand.

We sang " 'Tis a Gift to Be Simple" and "Chairs to Mend" from the Finchley-Read fifth-grade assembly program.

We sang better than we ever had. Mrs. Forrest would have been very proud.

Our singing was like magic.

It brought us together.

It made us friends.

Best of all, it emptied the apartment of my sisters' party.

Even my sisters seemed glad.

"Good-bye," Anitra waved, "whoever you are." Then she grabbed me and twirled me around. "Wow! What a scene. Jaded said he'd bring five, and he brought forty."

Pippa took out the Pin-the-Tail-on-the-Donkey. Anitra did the blindfolds and spun us. Christi won. We all played Musical Chairs while Anitra banged on her drums. Then we ate up the pink heart-shaped cake and drank all the punch. Nobody wanted to go home, but Mrs. Dildine came for Linda and offered lifts. After they all left, I found the nosegays in the refrigerator.

"If Mom sees them, she'll think nobody came to my party," I said.

♥ *Chapter Six*

Sunday we slept late and then cleaned up the apartment. It took all afternoon. Anitra cried a little when she found some of her favorite records scratched.

"Somebody used Daddy's razor," Pippa groaned.

"Somebody stole my perfume," Anitra sighed.

"I didn't know how we'd ever get rid of them."

They both looked at me. "Rosy did."

I couldn't believe it — for the second time in two days we weren't "them and me."

Around five o'clock Christi McCurry called me on the house phone and asked me to come over. If I kept a diary I could have immortalized the event in it. "What's it all about?" I said.

"We need to talk to you."

"We?"

I put on lots of Alluring Rose and some cheek toner and a few of Anitra's Luscious Lashes for good measure. I left the apartment without my sisters' seeing me. When I got to Christi's, she led me into her bedroom. Mari and Natali were on the bean bag chairs.

Something was up.

"We're putting together a new group and we'd like you to join us. Our goal is to get in touch with where we are and who we are right now."

"What do you need a group for?"

"You don't have to get so snippy, Rose."

Snippy? I wasn't snippy. I was furious. "Because of you and your Christi-Belles I went around for one miserable month trying to attract a bunch of boys to my party. Because of you calling me a Baby, I felt like one. I threw that stupid party that nearly wrecked my house, and then had to spend one whole day cleaning up the mess. All because of you and the Christi-Belles."

"Then you don't want to join the Christi-Belles?" Mari seemed shocked.

"The whole class can be in it," Christi said fast, "and nobody has to change her name."

"What else?" I said.

86

"No teasing," she said.

"I'll think about it," I said. Then I noticed her dresser crammed with tubes and jars. "If you'll show me how to put on that stuff."

"Makeup," she gasped. "What for? Christi-Belles won't need to pretend to be older. We won't have to party like the Putrids. We aren't up to that yet."

"But when we are, we *Super*-Babes should know how to do it."

"I see your point," Christi agreed slowly. I could also see that she was staring at my mouth and my eyelashes. But that didn't bother me. I thought we were more or less even.

When I got home, Mom and Dad were back, and my sisters were setting the table for seven. "Uncle Ralph and Aunt Teddy are coming for dinner," Dad said. "Mom and I picked up some Chinese food on the way home."

As soon as he came in the door, Uncle Ralph took out his camera and began adjusting his light meter. "Now for a few family shots," he said. "Last time we got together nobody was really in the mood."

Mom and Dad and Pippa and Anitra and me and Pie all got together behind the container of Moo Shoo Shrimp.

Uncle Ralph started snapping.

"Hey, sis, I have an idea for a new book on the kids."

"Rage and Rebellion in the Adolescent Child?"

"Growth and Change in the Family," he said as if it were an inspiration. "Can you think of anything better?"

"How about leaving us untitled for a while, Ralph," Mom said.

"Untitled?" He looked confused. "I don't get it. You've got to have a title, otherwise nobody knows what they're getting into."

Daddy began to laugh. He looked from
Anitra to Pippa to me. "That's just the
point," he said.

And we all had to agree.